There Was an Old DRAGON Who Swallowed a Knight

Penny Parker Klostermann

illustrated by Ben Mantle

Random House 🏠 New York

Library of Congress Cataloging-in-Publication Data
Klostermann, Penny Parker.
There was an old dragon who swallowed a knight / Penny Parker Klostermann ;
illustrated by Ben Mantle. — First edition.
pages cm.
Summary: In this variation on the traditional cumulative rhyme, a greedy,
hungry dragon eventually learns moderation.
ISBN 978-0-385-39080-4 (trade) — ISBN 978-0-375-97355-0 (lib. bdg.) —
ISBN 978-0-385-39081-1 (ebook)
1. Folk songs, English—Texts. [1. Folk songs. 2. Nonsense verses.]
I. Mantle, Ben, illustrator. II. Title.
PZ8.3.K693The 2015 782.42—dc23 [E] 2014026249

MANUFACTURED IN CHINA
10 9 8 7 6 5
First Edition

With love, for my parents, Wallace and Naomi Parker

—P.P.K.

For Myla Belle Pearce

—B.M.

There was an old dragon
who swallowed a **knight**.
I don't know why he swallowed the knight.

It's not polite!

There was an old dragon
who swallowed a **steed**
That galloped around at a terrible speed.
Oh, how the dragon wished it would stop,

That clippity, clippity, clippity, clop.

He swallowed the steed right after the knight.
I don't know why he swallowed the knight.

It's not
polite!

There was an old dragon
who swallowed a **squire**,

Who hollered, "That's hot!"
when the dragon breathed fire.

He swallowed the squire to calm the steed
That galloped around at a terrible speed.
He swallowed the steed right after the knight.
I don't know why he swallowed the knight.

It's not polite!

clippity, clippity, clippity, clop

There was an old dragon
who swallowed a cook—
A savory cook and his recipe book.

He swallowed the cook to fatten the squire.
He swallowed the squire to calm the steed
That galloped around at a terrible speed.
He swallowed the steed right after the knight.
I don't know why he swallowed the knight.

It's not
polite!

clippity, clippity,
clippity, clop

There was an old dragon
who swallowed a lady.
It seems quite shady
he'd swallow a lady.

He swallowed the lady to rule the cook.
He swallowed the cook to fatten the squire.
He swallowed the squire to calm the steed
That galloped around at a terrible speed.
He swallowed the steed right after the knight.
I don't know why he swallowed the knight.

It's not polite!

clippity, clippity, clippity, clop

There was an old dragon
who swallowed a castle,
Swallowed it down to the last golden tassel.

He swallowed the castle
to hold the lady.

He swallowed the lady
to rule the cook.

He swallowed the cook
to fatten the squire.

He swallowed the squire
to calm the steed
That galloped around
at a terrible speed.

clippity, clippity, clippity, clop

He swallowed the steed
right after the knight.
I don't know why he
swallowed the knight.

It's not polite!

There was an old dragon
who swallowed a **moat**,

Guzzled and gulped it
right down his throat.

With all of that water, he started to bloat.
And that's when the dragon roared, and I quote:

"Okay, enough! I've had enough—
More than enough of this swallowing stuff!

Maybe I've been a tad impolite.
Perchance I should only
          have swallowed the knight."

So he burped out the moat
That had caused him to bloat.
He burped out the castle,
Along with the tassel.
He burped out the lady
(Who found that quite shady).
He burped out the cook
And his recipe book.
He burped out the squire,
Now blackened with fire.

Then, with all of the power that he could amass,
The dragon burped out one last billow of gas.

BUR

RRRRR 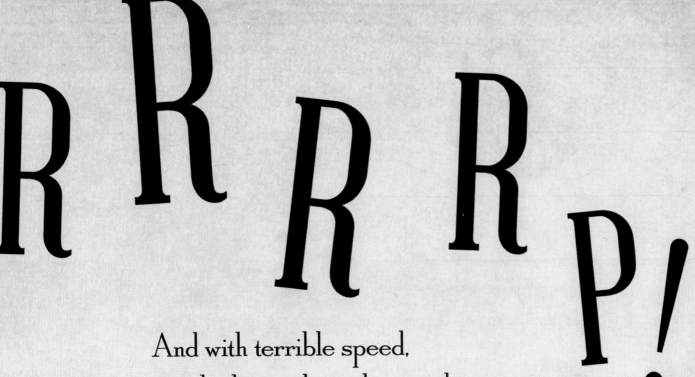 P!

And with terrible speed,
he burped out the steed.

Clippity, clippity, clippity, clop.
Clippity, clippity, clippity—STOP!

There was an old dragon
who swallowed a knight.

Ahhh . . . just right.
"Good knight!"

clippity, clippity, clippity, clop